The Christmas Present Mystery

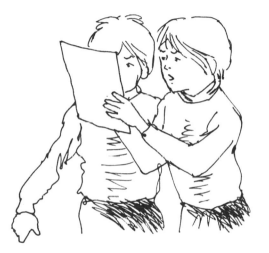

by Marion M. Markham

Illustrated by Emily Arnold McCully

Houghton Mifflin Company   Boston   1984

Library of Congress Cataloging in Publication Data

Markham, Marion M.
  The Christmas present mystery.

  Summary: Twin sisters Mickey and Kate combine their
skills to discover the explanation for a mysterious face
that has appeared in a family photograph.
  [1. Mystery and detective stories. 2. Twins — Fiction.
3. Christmas — Fiction. 4. Photography — Fiction]
I. McCully, Emily Arnold, ill. II. Title.
PZ7.M33946Ch 1984   [Fic]   84-4557
ISBN 0-395-36383-7

85003054 -52

Contents

1 · The Mysterious Face

It was December 24. The Dixon family was boarding the boat to Indian Island. They were going to spend Christmas with Uncle Corwin. He was the chief of police on the island.

Eleven-year-old Kate Dixon carried packages wrapped in brightly colored paper. Her twin sister, Mickey, held a large brown envelope. Inside the envelope was their Christmas gift to Uncle Corwin — a photograph of the family. It hadn't been ready until this morning. The twins had picked it up on the way to the boat. They were going to wrap it when they got to Uncle Corwin's house.

Mrs. Dixon juggled her purse and an armload of Christmas presents. Jeff, the twins' big brother, carried the suitcases.

Miss Amanda Wink, the Dixons' next-door neighbor, was going with them. "Are you sure I won't be in the way?" she said.

"Corwin is expecting you," Mother said. "His housekeeper, Mrs. Sage, is spending Christmas on the mainland. You'll sleep in her room."

Below their feet the boat engines pounded. Out on deck a whistle tooted. The boat slowly backed away from the shore.

Miss Wink began working on her knitting.

Kate read a photography book. She was hoping to get a camera for Christmas. The family photograph for Uncle Corwin had been her idea.

"Let's look at the picture," said Mickey.

Miss Wink said, "I hope it turned out well." She had taken the picture with Mother's camera.

Mickey opened the brown envelope. She stared at the picture.

"Something's wrong," she said.

"Oh, dear me," said Miss Wink.

Everyone looked over Mickey's shoulder.

In the picture Mother, Jeff, and the twins were sitting on the couch the way they had been when Miss Wink took the picture. But looking over Mother's shoulder was another face. A boy with dark eyes and long dark bangs looked directly into the camera. He had his tongue stuck out.

"A ghost," said Miss Wink. Sometimes Miss Wink had strange ideas. Mother said it was because she had lived alone since her parents retired to Florida.

Kate said, "I don't believe in ghosts. There has to be a scientific explanation." Kate was very interested in science.

"No science, please," Jeff said. "I'd like to enjoy Christmas without you showing off."

"But she's right," Mickey said. "It's too bad we didn't look in the envelope before we left the camera store. We might have talked to the clerk and solved the mystery." Mickey was going to be a detective.

Opening her suitcase, she took out a magnifying glass and studied the picture again.

"Let me have a look," Kate said.

"See anything?" Jeff asked.

"No," Kate and Mickey answered together.

Miss Wink said, "Perhaps he's a poltergeist?"

"What's that?" Mickey wanted to know.

"A poltergeist is a mischievous spirit," said Miss Wink.

Mother said, "I think you're right about one thing, Amanda. This is a boy with a mischievous spirit."

"But why did he do it?" said Jeff.

"And how?" said Mickey.

Kate said, "There must be a scientific explanation."

2 · Clues and Questions

"Let's look at the clues," Mickey said.

Kate took the negative out of the envelope. She held it up.

"The first clue is that the boy's face is not in the negative."

Mickey looked at the negative too. "You're right," she said.

Kate looked at the photograph again.

"The second clue is that the lamp doesn't show in the picture. The boy's head is in front of it."

Mickey said, "That's not a clue."

"Yes it is," Kate said. "We just don't know what it means."

"Any more?"

"Several," said Kate. "We'd better make a list."

When they were finished, their list had four clues and two questions.

CLUES

1. The boy's head is in the photograph but not in the negative.

2. The head in the picture hides the lamp that is in the negative.

3. The photograph is larger than the negative.

4. ACME PHOTOLAB is stamped on the back of the photograph.

QUESTIONS

1. How did the face get in the photograph?

2. Why was it done?

Mickey didn't think that the third clue was important.

"It tells us that the picture was printed in an enlarger," said Kate.

Mickey said, "If I had my Junior Detective

Fingerprint Set, I could dust the negative and the picture for fingerprints." A Junior Detective Fingerprint Set was what Mickey wanted for Christmas.

"What good would that do?" Kate asked.

"It would help us identify the boy."

Kate said, "We already have a picture to identify him. This isn't a mystery that can be solved with fingerprints. It's going to take scientific reasoning."

"You're the scientist," said Mickey. "How did the face get in the picture?"

"I'm not sure. One way would be to put two negatives in the enlarger at the same time. But I think that would look like a double exposure. We'd see the lamp *and* the boy's face."

She looked at the index in her photography book. There was nothing there about putting faces where they didn't belong.

Mother said, "You'll have to wait until you get back home to solve this mystery. In the meantime, we'll have to get another gift."

"What a bother," Miss Wink said. Her ball

of red yarn slipped off her lap. As she bent to pick it up, the boat rolled and one knitting needle fell to the floor.

"Oh, dear me," she said, "Now I've dropped a stitch in Uncle Corwin's Christmas muffler."

Mickey picked up the knitting needle. Jeff chased the yarn ball that had unrolled across the cabin floor. He began rewinding it.

Kate said, "We'll find something else for Uncle Corwin."

Mickey said, "And we'll solve the mystery of the face."

"I hope so," Miss Wink said.

Mother patted Miss Wink's hand. "Don't worry, Amanda. You're almost finished with the scarf."

Miss Wink took out a tape measure and stretched it along her knitting. "So I am," she said.

Jeff handed Miss Wink her yarn and then went to look out the porthole.

"We're there," he said.

Uncle Corwin was waiting for them on the boat dock. He put the suitcases and Christmas packages in his police car.

Except for the police car and an ambulance, there were no cars anywhere on Indian Island. Most people had bicycles. Or walked. Or rode horses.

Uncle Corwin had a horse named Spice that was trained to do tricks. Once, he and Spice had worked in a traveling "Wild West" show. When the show closed, he wanted to keep Spice. The Indian Island Village Board wanted a police chief who could ride a horse.

Kate explained, "We have some Christmas shopping to do."

"We'll walk to your house when we're done," Mickey said.

3 · The Empty Store

Main Street was only ten blocks long. In summer it was crowded with tourists. Now the street was empty. Most of the stores were empty too.

Kate and Mickey walked past the silent stores looking for a place where they could buy a Christmas present for Uncle Corwin.

Mickey said, "Maybe we can get him some saltwater taffy."

"Good idea," Kate said. But when they got to the candy shop, it too was closed.

"Your turn to think of something," said Mickey.

Kate didn't answer. She was looking in the window next door.

During the summer, the store was rented by a photographer. He took funny pictures of people. The photographer was gone, but he had left some things behind.

Next to the glass front door was a large painting of a man wearing a coonskin cap. He was fighting a grizzly bear. There was a hole where the man's head should have been. People put their heads through the hole, and the photographer took their pictures.

"I think I know how it could be done," Kate said.

"How what could be done?" Mickey asked.

"How a face that isn't in the negative could be printed in the photograph."

"I knew your scientific mind would figure it out," said Mickey.

Kate said, "Let's go to the drugstore and see Mr. Chin. He sells film and develops pictures."

4 · Mr. Chin's Clue

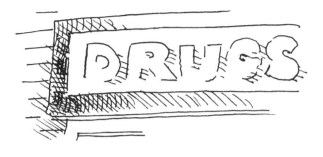

Mr. Chin's drugstore was really two stores. One half was an ordinary drugstore. The other half was a Chinese drugstore for the fishermen who lived on the island.

Mr. Chin was on the Chinese side filling a prescription. Instead of counting pills, he was weighing dried leaves. And instead of putting them into a bottle, he put them into a large, brown paper bag.

"Bring two quarts of water to a boil, Mrs. Han," he explained. "Turn the stove off and slowly add these leaves to the water. Let them soak for two hours. Then strain and drink a half cup before every meal."

When the woman left, Mickey said, "Hello,
Mr. Chin."

Mr. Chin squinted through his glasses.
Then he smiled. "The Dixon twins. I did not
know you at first. You have grown since last
summer."

Kate said, "Do those dried leaves really do
any good?"

"Many generations have used them to cure illness. Do you wish a Chinese prescription?"

"No," Mickey said. "Information. Do you know the Acme Photolab?"

"Yes. They used to develop all the film my customers brought in."

"But they don't now?" Mickey asked.

"It was too slow — sending the film to the mainland on the boat. The summer visitors do not like to wait. Last year I put in a darkroom here. That way I can give prompt service."

Kate asked, "Do you develop and print the pictures yourself?"

"Usually. When it is very busy, I hire someone to help me."

"Then you'd know if my idea would work."

"What idea?" Mr. Chin said.

"Suppose I wanted to add something to a picture that wasn't in the original negative," Kate said. "A face, for example."

Mr. Chin nodded.

"Could I put the negative and the photographic paper under the enlarger with a circle of cardboard blocking out part of the picture? I'd expose the negative. Then I'd use another piece of cardboard to cover the section I'd already exposed. And I'd put a negative of someone's face in the spot that had been covered before and then expose that."

Mr. Chin thought. "I have never done that. But, yes, I think it would work."

"I think so too."

Mr. Chin said. "I sometimes have trouble reading the characters in a Chinese prescription, so I have a very powerful magnifying glass with a light. If I used it to look at the photograph I might be able to see something." He took them behind the counter.

Mickey handed him the picture.

"David!" Mr. Chin sounded surprised.

"You know him?"

"Yes. He helped in my darkroom last summer. Your uncle did not recognize him?"

Kate said, "The photograph was to be a Christmas surprise for Uncle Corwin."

"David is the nephew of his housekeeper,"
Mr. Chin said.

"Mrs. Sage?" said Kate.

Mickey asked, "Do you know where he is
now?"

"I have not seen him since his family left
the island in September," said Mr. Chin.

Mr. Chin studied the photograph under his
magnifying glass. He said, "I see nothing un-
usual. I am sorry I cannot help."

"You have helped," Kate said.

"Yes," said Mickey. "Now we know who the boy is."

Before they left, the twins bought some after-shave lotion for Uncle Corwin.

As he wrapped the package, Mr. Chin said, "David's father was the photographer who took funny pictures of the summer visitors."

"In the store down the street?" Kate asked.

"Yes."

"We know three things about the boy," Mickey said when they were outside. "His name is David, he knows photography, and Mrs. Sage is his aunt."

Mickey said, "Let's ask Uncle Corwin if he knows where David is now."

5 · The Search

Kate poked Mickey. "Look."

Mickey turned around. A tall boy in a red plaid jacket was crossing Main Street.

"That's him," Kate whispered loudly. "David."

"It can't be," said Mickey.

Kate said, "I'm sure of it. I got a good look at his face."

"What would he be doing here?"

"Let's ask him. He cut through over there." Kate pointed to a narrow walk between the empty candy shop and the photographer's store.

Snow had drifted between the buildings.

Mickey bent down. "No fresh footprints," she said. "The snow's frozen too hard."

The deserted walkway behind the stores was lined with padlocked doors.

"This is spooky," Kate said. "It's like being in a ghost town."

"Where else would you look for a ghost?"

"That boy wasn't a ghost."

"Of course," said Mickey. "He's a real boy. And he's somewhere on the island. We just have to find him."

"How?"

Mickey said, "Maybe he's hiding in one of these empty stores."

"But they're all locked."

"Not this one," Mickey said, pointing to an open padlock.

"I don't think we ought to go in. Not without Uncle Corwin."

"By the time we get Uncle Corwin, it'll be too late." Mickey opened the door quietly. Stepping inside, she could see that it was the photographer's store. Kate walked in behind her.

The boy was looking out the front window.

He didn't seem to know that Mickey and Kate were there. Then a strong gust of wind caught the open back door. It banged shut.

He turned. The only light was from the window behind him, and they couldn't see his face.

"Who are you?" he said. He sounded scared.

"Don't be afraid," Kate said.

Mickey said, "We just want to talk to you."

The boy didn't answer. Instead he backed toward the front door. It was ajar.

"We want to know why your face is in our photograph," Kate said.

The boy opened the front door and ran outside. Kate and Mickey followed. He ran across the street, cutting around the stores and up a hill. By the time Mickey and Kate had climbed to the top, the boy had disappeared into some woods.

Kate was breathless. "Too bad Jeff isn't here," she panted. "He would have caught him."

Mickey didn't want to give up now that they were so close. But the woods were very dark and the snow looked deep. Because the woods got very little sunlight, the snow never melted until spring.

"Let's talk to Uncle Corwin," she said. "Perhaps he'll know where David's family is."

6 · Miss Wink Screams

Uncle Corwin's house was also his office. The police headquarters was in the living room. On the front door, just below the sign that said INDIAN ISLAND POLICE, was a Christmas wreath with a big red bow.

As the twins walked into the house, they heard Miss Wink scream. They ran to the kitchen.

Miss Wink said, "The poltergeist was looking at me. Through the window."

"He must have followed us," said Kate.

Uncle Corwin came out of his office.

"What poltergeist?" he said.

"Th-th-there," Miss Wink stuttered. She pointed toward the kitchen window.

Uncle Corwin ran outside, and the twins followed. Mickey saw a flash of red plaid disappear into the barn.

Kate shouted, "We have him trapped now." She was wrong. The barn door opened. Spice galloped out. The boy in the red plaid coat was riding bareback. He had his arms wrapped around Spice's neck.

"Twee-tee-dee-dee," whistled Uncle Corwin. Spice halted suddenly. The horse knelt down. The boy jumped off as the horse started to roll over.

Miss Wink was just coming out of the house. "How did you make him do that?" she said.

"Spice used to do tricks in a 'Wild West' show," Mickey said.

Uncle Corwin called, "Stop right there."

The boy turned. His chin was stuck out, and he tried to stand tall. But Mickey thought she saw tears in his eyes.

"David!" Uncle Corwin sounded surprised.

Miss Wink said, "Who is he?"

Uncle Corwin said, "David's father is Mrs. Sage's brother."

"Who's Mrs. Sage?" Miss Wink asked.

Kate said, "Uncle Corwin's housekeeper. Don't you remember?"

Miss Wink said, "Sometimes I forget things."

There was a loud whistling sound from the kitchen.

Miss Wink frowned. "Like the tea kettle," she said. "Oh dear me. I hope it hasn't boiled dry."

"If it was dry, there wouldn't be any steam to make it whistle," Kate said. But Miss Wink was already in the house and didn't hear her.

Uncle Corwin took David's arm. "Let's go inside," he said.

David said, "Where's Auntie Sage?" His voice was trembling.

Uncle Corwin said, "She's away, David. But you're welcome in my house."

7 · Why David Ran Away

Everyone, including David, followed Miss Wink into the kitchen. Mother and Jeff were already there.

"Who would like peanut-butter-and-jelly sandwiches?" Miss Wink asked.

Mickey said, "We all would."

"And cambric tea?" said Miss Wink.

David said, "My mother makes cambric tea."

Jeff asked, "What is it?"

"Hot water with milk and sugar in it." Miss Wink poured water from the kettle into china tea cups.

"I think I'll add a little coffee to mine," said Uncle Corwin.

Miss Wink passed a plate of sandwiches cut into quarters. David gobbled down each one in a single bite. When the plate was empty, he took a sip of his cambric tea.

Suddenly he seemed to realize that no one else was eating.

"Was that supposed to be for everyone?" he asked.

Kate said, "Miss Wink isn't used to cooking for a family."

David said, "I'm sorry. I haven't eaten anything since yesterday morning."

"It won't take me long to fix more sandwiches," said Miss Wink. She began cutting the crusts off the slices of white bread.

Uncle Corwin said, "Where are your parents, David?"

"Mother's on the mainland. In the city. I don't know where my father is."

Then Mickey said, "What happened to your father?"

David explained that his parents had had an argument. His father wanted to travel with a carnival so he could make enough money to buy a better camera. His mother didn't want to go. So his father went alone.

Mickey said, "And you got an after-school job at the Acme Photolab?"

"Yes. Until yesterday. When I ran away." He said the last words very softly.

David sniffed back tears. "Dad said he'd

only be gone for a month or so. Then he was going to open a photographic studio in the city. He wanted to take pictures of people."

"Last summer he was taking pictures of people," said Kate.

"Funny pictures. But he wanted to do wedding pictures and real portraits. Maybe even news pictures for the paper and TV."

"Why did you spoil our family photograph?" Jeff asked.

"What photograph?" Uncle Corwin said.

Mickey poked Jeff. "You've ruined the surprise," she said.

"This was going to be your Christmas present," Kate said. She gave Uncle Corwin the picture.

"I don't understand," he said.

"We didn't either at first," Mickey said. "Then Kate figured it out, and we went to ask Mr. Chin if she was right."

"Whoa," Uncle Corwin said. "Not so fast. You can tell me later. Now I think we'd better call David's mother. I'm sure she's worried."

"I'm sorry about that," David said. "I wasn't running away from her."

"But she probably thinks you were," Mother said.

David thought for a moment. "I guess I was really trying to get away from Christmas."

Miss Wink said, "It can be a very lonely time if you're not with people you love." The twins knew she was thinking about her own parents in Florida.

"I mean," David said, "in the lab I was printing family Christmas card pictures. And I didn't even know where to send my father a

card. It was like I didn't have a family any-more."

Kate said, "So that's why you ruined our Christmas photograph. You wanted to put yourself in someone's family for Christmas."

David said, "I didn't exactly think about it that way. But I guess you're right."

Miss Wink put down a new plate of sand-wiches.

Uncle Corwin came back from his office.

"Your father's on the telephone, David. He wants to talk to you."

David's eyes lit up. "Where is he?" he said.

"He's with your mother. He came home for Christmas. With a new camera. They've been very worried about you."

Uncle Corwin took David to the telephone.

When they came back, David had a big grin on his face. "I'm going to have a family Christmas after all."

"There isn't another boat until morning, so David will sleep here with us," Uncle Corwin said.

Mother said, "And you can have Christmas Eve dinner with us tonight."

"After all those peanut-butter sandwiches?" Miss Wink asked.

"Have you ever noticed how much Jeff eats?" said Mickey.

"David can help trim the Christmas tree too," Kate said.

8 · Christmas Eve

"I'm sorry I spoiled your Christmas surprise,"
David told the twins.

"We're not," they said together.

"It gave us a mystery to solve," Mickey said.

"And I figured out how to combine two
negatives in one photograph," Kate added.

David said, "I'll print a new picture for you
next week. Without my face in it this time."

"Now that we've settled that," Uncle Corwin
said, "let's trim the Christmas tree."

Later, at dinner, David seemed to be just as

hungry as if he hadn't eaten a plate of peanut-butter-and-jelly sandwiches two hours before. He ate a whole turkey drumstick and three helpings of stuffing.

"A fantastic meal," said Uncle Corwin. He patted his stomach to show that he was full.

Mother smiled. "Thank you."

Mickey swallowed her last spoonful of peppermint-candy ice cream. There was one Christmas cookie left on her saucer. It looked delicious. But she was too full to eat another bite. She broke the cookie in two and gave a half each to David and Jeff.

After dinner, Mother let everyone open one Christmas present.

Miss Wink gave Mother and David jars of homemade quince jelly. And she promised Uncle Corwin that his red wool scarf would be finished by Christmas morning.

Jeff got the baseball catcher's mitt he'd asked for. Kate got her camera, and Mickey her Junior Detective Fingerprint Set.

"Just right for two young detectives," Uncle Corwin said.

Miss Wink said, "Between you girls and my cat, I feel so much safer these days."

"I didn't know you had a cat," said Uncle Corwin.

"I decided I needed a pet to watch my house."

"A watch cat?" David said.

"A Scratch Cat. I thought about a parakeet, to tell me if someone came in. Then I decided on a cat. Better protection."

Uncle Corwin said, "A cat is better than a parakeet." He could barely hide his smile.

"I just thought of something," Kate said. "When you saw the face in the window, you didn't faint the way you sometimes do when you're scared."

"Oh dear me, you're right," Miss Wink said. "It was scary. I hadn't thought about it before."

And she fainted.

"Gosh," David said. "I never meant to scare anyone."

Kate said, "Don't worry about it. Miss Wink likes to faint."

Miss Wink sat up. "Not exactly. I guess it's just a habit."

David said, "I have an idea. When we all get back to the city, why don't I come over some day and take a picture of all of you. Including Miss Wink and Scratch Cat."

"Great idea," Mickey said.

Kate said, "We'll all want a copy of that photograph."